Watch out!
I am Hoot Owl!
I am hungry.

And here I come!

HOOT OWL, MAS

ILLUSTRATED BY

Sean Taylor

Jean Jullien

To James—for taking Hoot Owl
under his wing!

S. T.

I dedicate this book to Sarah, who
is as cute as Hoot; to my papa and
my maman, who read me stories that
inspired me; and to Mélane and Nico,
who grew up to them with me

J. J.

CANDLEWICK PRESS

Text copyright © 2014 by Sean Taylor * Illustrations copyright © 2014 by Jean Jullien * All rights reserved *
No part of this book may be reproduced, transmitted, or stored in an information retrieval system in
any form or by any means, graphic, electronic, or mechanical, including photocopying, taping, and
recording, without prior written permission from the publisher * First U.S. edition 2015 * Library of Congress
Catalog Card Number 2013957281 * ISBN 978-0-7636-7578-3 * This book was typeset in Futura *
Candlewick Press, 99 Dover Street, Somerville, Massachusetts 02144 * visit us at www.candlewick.com *
Printed in Shenzhen, Guangdong, China * 14 15 16 17 18 19 CCP 10 9 8 7 6 5 4 3 2 1

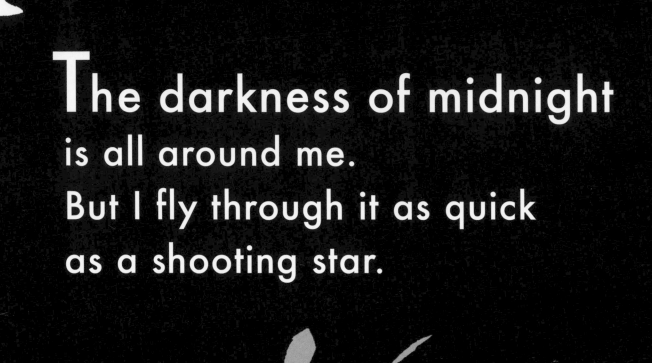

The darkness of midnight
is all around me.
But I fly through it as quick
as a shooting star.

a tasty rabbit for me to eat.
Soon my sharp beak will be
gobbling that rabbit up!

Everyone knows
owls are wise.
But as well as
being wise,
I am a master
of disguise.

I devise a costume.

Look—

I disguise myself as . . .

a delicious carrot.

And here I come!

The night has
a thousand eyes,
and two of them
are mine.
I swoop through
the bleak blackness
like a wolf in the air.

And look there . . .

a juicy little lamb stands, helpless,
in the cool of the night!

The lamb looks cuddly,
but soon I will be eating it.

Everyone knows owls are wise.
But as well as being wise,

I am a master of disguise.
I devise a costume.

Look—

I disguise myself as . . .

a soft and fluffy mother sheep.

It is the perfect way to catch a lamb.

I wait.

The terrible silence of the
night spreads everywhere.
But I cut through it like a knife.

And look there . . .

a pigeon stands,
trembling,
afraid that
a dangerous
creature-of-the-dark,
such as an owl,
might be passing by!

In a matter of moments,
the pigeon will be
in my tummy.

BIRD-BATH

Everyone knows
owls are wise.
But as well as
being wise,
I am a master
of disguise.

I devise a costume.

Look—

I disguise myself as . . .

an ornamental
birdbath.

It is the
perfect way
to catch a
pigeon.

I wait.

It doesn't work.   But never mind!

I am Hoot Owl!
I am very, very hungry.

The shadowy night stretches away forever, as black as burnt toast.

And look there . . .

a mouth-watering pizza!

My eyes glitter like sardines
because I am sure the pizza will be mine.

Everyone knows owls are wise.
But as well as being wise,

I am a master
of disguise.

a waiter!

It is the perfect way
to catch a pizza.

I wait.

They don't call me
Master of Disguise
for nothing.

I chomp the pizza with my deadly-dangerous beak.

It is pepperoni.

The last bite is as good as the first.

Then, tired but satisfied,
I transform myself
back into plain Hoot Owl.

I disappear into the dark
enormousness of the night.

I am gone.

And the
world
can sleep
again.

Until
Hoot Owl
returns.